S0-BOM-182

ARTHUR'S LAST STAND

THE ARTHUR BOOKS

Railroad Arthur
Arthur the Kid
Buffalo Arthur
The Lone Arthur
Klondike Arthur
Arthur's Last Stand

★ ALAN COREN ★

Weekly Reader Books presents

ARTHUR'S LAST STAND

Illustrated by John Astrop

Little, Brown and Company
Boston   Toronto

This book is a presentation of
Weekly Reader Books.

Weekly Reader Books offers book clubs for children
from preschool through junior high school.
All quality hardcover books are selected by
a distinguished Weekly Reader Selection Board.

For further information write to:
Weekly Reader Books
1250 Fairwood Ave.
Columbus, Ohio 43216

COPYRIGHT © 1977 BY ALAN COREN

ALL RIGHTS RESERVED. NO PART OF THIS BOOK MAY BE REPRODUCED IN ANY FORM
OR BY ANY ELECTRONIC OR MECHANICAL MEANS INCLUDING INFORMATION STOR-
AGE AND RETRIEVAL SYSTEMS WITHOUT PERMISSION IN WRITING FROM THE PUB-
LISHER, EXCEPT BY A REVIEWER WHO MAY QUOTE BRIEF PASSAGES IN A REVIEW.

Library of Congress Cataloging in Publication Data

Coren, Alan, 1938–
    Arthur's last stand.

    SUMMARY: Ten-year-old Arthur employs an unusual
technique to save the garrison at Fort Moccasin from an
Indian attack.
    [1. The West—Fiction. 2. Indians of North America—
Fiction] I. Astrop, John. II. Title.
PZ7.C81538As   1977   [Fic]   79–14052
ISBN 0–316–15742–2

PRINTED IN THE UNITED STATES OF AMERICA

For Tobias, Jemima, and Joshua

★

ONCE upon a time, about a hundred years ago, there stood a fort in the very middle of what is now the state of Montana but then was called the Territory of Montana.

The fort was surrounded by mountains. Indeed, there was very little in Montana that was not surrounded by mountains. That was why, as you've probably guessed, it was called Montana. For not only did the great Rocky Mountains run right through the center of the territory, but more than a dozen other smaller ranges crisscrossed and wandered and sprouted there. All of them had wonderful names, like the Crazy Mountains, and Flathead Range, the Bitterroot Range, the Whitefish Range, and both the Little Belt Mountains *and* the Big Belt Mountains. Within these great saw-toothed, snow-crowned ranges, individual mountains, too, had (and still have) marvelous names of their own. So that if you want to see exactly where this particular fort stood, look on a map of the United States, find Montana, and look for a mountain called Bear Paw Mountain.

Bear Paw Mountain rose up behind the fort, and in front of the fort ran Milk River. Across Milk River, on the Canadian border, rose the mountain called Old Man on His Back Plateau, which the sentry posted on the highest lookout point of the fort could just see through his telescope.

There was always a sentry up there, of

course. His telescope was always out, and the sharp mountain sun would always wink off its bright brass bands, because it was a very clean telescope indeed.

It was that sort of fort. Or, more to the point, it had that sort of commanding officer in charge of it; whatever else people might have said about Major Oliver Spoongurgle, they had to admit that Fort Moccasin was the classiest, cleanest garrison in the entire U.S. cavalry.

And people *did* say other things about him, especially his men. That was hardly surprising,

for Major Oliver Spoongurgle kept them hard at it, day and night, painting and polishing and cleaning. The high, wooden walls of the fort gleamed the rich brown gleam of fine furniture. The gravel of its inner courtyard was rolled and swept into stripes until it resembled a yellow lawn; and on that gravel, the neat mounds of cannonballs that stood beside the

4

sparkling guns might have been made of gold, not iron, for all the care that had gone into making them shine.

As for the horses in the freshly painted stables, they would have looked more at home in a circus than in an army. Their manes were braided and set off with yellow-and-blue bows (to match the men's uniforms), yellow-and-gold

5

braid trimmed their tails, and every strap and buckle was decorated with the kind of twinkling ornament that would, no doubt, have done very well had they been pulling a royal coach, but had very little place on a battlefield.

The cavalrymen themselves spent more time in shining their boots than in sharpening their swords, and more time in polishing their buttons than in practicing with their rifles, and more time in fancy marching than in battle training. So it was quite understandable that from time to time the men would pause in their polishing or their sewing or their ironing to wonder just why it was that their commanding officer was so crazy about neatness; and the only conclusion they ever came to was that it must have been something to do with his name. If you were named Oliver Spoongurgle, they argued, you had to do everything just a little bit better than if you were called, say, John Smith, since people, being the way they are, don't need much of an excuse to start making fun of someone named Spoongurgle.

What the men didn't know, however, and what worried them more than anything, was whether the major was any good at fighting. For that was why Fort Moccasin had been built, after all, and that was why the cavalry was manning it.

Because these were pretty grim days in Montana. Just a year or so earlier, the Sioux, who were probably the bravest and the toughest of all the Indian tribes, had won their greatest victory over the United States Army. A few hundred miles away, at the Little Bighorn, the Sioux had wiped out five companies of the crack Seventh Cavalry, including their general, George Armstrong Custer. Afterward, though expedition after expedition was mounted by the army, though battle after battle was fought, they never succeeded in capturing Sitting Bull, chief of the Sioux.

Even worse, from the army's point of view, was that the warriors of many other tribes — the Oglala, the Miniconjou, and the Blackfoot — had joined forces with Sitting Bull.

Under their great fighting chiefs (men like
Black Moon, No Neck, Iron Dog, Big Road,
and Spotted Eagle), they rode out time after
time to raid the forts and the villages and the
wagon trains of Montana and Idaho and
Dakota.

Which was why, at the end of the 1870s, so
many new forts had been hurriedly built,
strung out across these states; but with so many
new forts, the U.S. Army was stretched very
thin. Few of the forts held more than a hundred
men. Since the Indian raiding parties often
contained up to a thousand fine riders, who
were not only crack shots but also clever tacti-
cians who could plan and fight a battle as well
as their blue-coated cavalry enemies, it isn't

difficult to understand why Major Oliver Spoongurgle's men sometimes felt a worried shiver pass through them when they saw him holding meetings with his junior officers to discuss new curtains. He ought, perhaps, to have been working out battle tactics!

And of all the men, none worried more about what might happen when the Indians attacked than the cookhouse detail — that's to say, the three men who had to do all the dirty jobs around the fort kitchen: Private Bingle, who peeled potatoes, Private Conk, who washed the dishes, and Private Wibbley, who swept. They had not, of course, joined the cavalry in order to mess around in the kitchens, but that, unfortunately, was all that Major Oliver Spoongurgle would allow them to do.

They may not have made bad soldiers, or bad horsemen, or bad shots, but they never had the chance to find out, since the major would never allow them near guns or horses, simply because of their shapes. For Private Bingle was a head shorter than all the other men, and Pri-

vate Conk was a head taller than all the other men — except, of course, that he was two heads taller than Private Bingle — and as for Private Wibbley, he was fatter than any other three soldiers put together.

On the day when he took command of his company and lined them all up before him, Major Oliver Spoongurgle had taken one look at these three odd shapes who were completely spoiling the nice neat look of the line of men, and almost fainted from the shock!

"Uggh!" he shrieked, in a somewhat un-officer-like manner. "Who are those horrible, horrible men?"

"Troopers Bingle, Conk, and Wibbley, sir," replied the sergeant beside him.

"Troopers?" exclaimed Major Oliver Spoon-gurgle, dabbing at his face with his lavender-scented hankie. "*Troopers?* I'm not having them trooping with *me*, they're ruining the whole look of the column. I'd just as soon have three pigs put in uniforms to follow me about! This is going to be the most splendid company

11

in the entire United States cavalry. It's going to win all sorts of prizes; I'm not going to have it turned into a laughingstock by those three freaks. You're not to call them troopers, Sergeant, you're not, you're *not*, you're NOT!"

The sergeant looked at him for a bit, since he had never seen a major stamping his feet and jumping up and down before, but of course he did not say anything except: "Yes, sir, very good, sir. May I refer to them as privates, sir?"

The major sighed, and sniffed, and brushed a tiny speck of dust from his immaculate new uniform.

"Very well, if you must, you must. Personally, I get all hot and cold just thinking about them as soldiers at all. But keep them out of my sight, do you understand? If I see them again in my lovely fort, I shall probably scream."

After which Major Oliver Spoongurgle dismissed the men and went inside with his three junior officers to choose wallpaper. He left poor Bingle, Conk, and Wibbley to receive the wretched news that they were assigned to the

12

kitchen forever, in order that their commanding officer might never set eyes on them again.

That was why they were more worried than anyone about Indian attacks. They were allowed no guns with which to defend themselves, no horses on which they might escape, not even a sword. All that they had to fight with was a number of large potatoes that Bingle had managed to hide and that they planned to throw at any Indians who got close enough. They also had three of Wibbley's broomsticks to which they had tied three forks that Conk had borrowed from the kitchen one day, to use as spears.

Not that they had much confidence in them.

"You don't often hear," said Conk gloomily, when they'd finished tying the forks on, "of wars being won by the side with the biggest potatoes."

"I don't remember hearing about the Charge of the Fork Brigade, either," said Bingle.

Whereupon the three friends fell silent, thinking a number of terrifying thoughts and wondering how soon it would be before the thoughts turned into something worse.

They did not have long to wait.

Three days later, on an early April morning, as the clear air began to soften with spring, Chief Sitting Bull came across the Canadian border from the camp in which he had been planning his new campaign. He rode at the head of fifteen hundred warriors, and struck at villages along the Little Missouri River just two hundred miles east of Fort Moccasin.

All the forts in the area were put on immediate alert, and the battle plans of all the commanding officers swung into action. Except for those of Major Oliver Spoongurgle, who didn't have any.

He was in his new four-poster bed, admiring the color scheme he had chosen for his room, when his second-in-command, Captain Sam Sutton, burst in.

Major Oliver Spoongurgle sat up in bed excitedly.

"The goat!" he cried. "Has it arrived?"

"What?" said Captain Sam Sutton, taken by surprise.

"Our new regimental goat," snapped the major impatiently. "Our mascot! The finishing touch to my beautiful fort. The one thing every smart cavalry company must have, a big, beautiful, white goat, with lovely, long, curly horns, a goat to lead our processions when we ride out to —"

"It's no time to talk of goats, sir!" interrupted the captain. "Sitting Bull is on the warpath; he's wiped out two settlements along the

15

Little Missouri! Shall I muster the men while you dress, sir?"

"*What?*" shrieked Major Oliver Spoongurgle. "Are you mad? Are you asking me to ride out against the Poo without a proper mascot?"

"The *who?*" inquired the captain, staring at him.

"Not the Who," rapped the major, "the Poo!"

The captain closed his eyes in despair, and shook his head.

"I think you mean the *Sioux*, sir," he murmured, "don't you?"

"Poo, Who, Sioux, what difference does it make?" barked the major angrily. "The important thing is the goat. I have no intention of leaving this fort and marching anywhere until my goat arrives. I sent away for him two weeks ago, and until he turns up, we shall carry on as before."

"But, sir . . ."

"I rather thought," said Major Oliver Spoongurgle, sinking back against his yellow-and-blue silk pillows, "that we'd dress him in a blue horse-blanket with his name picked out in yellow embroidery. What do you say to that, Sutton?"

But the captain had already left.

And, I'm afraid to say, without even bothering to salute.

For the next two days, Sitting Bull's braves rampaged along the Little Missouri, skirmishing with settlers, raiding villages in lightning strikes, avoiding the pursuing cavalry companies dispatched from the various forts and garrisons, and generally growing more and more daring as they grew more and more successful in their attacks. The men of Fort Moccasin waited and sweated and prayed for orders and bit their nails. None of this made the slightest impression on their commanding officer, except, naturally, for the last mentioned.

"Bitten nails!" he yelled one morning, at early parade. "I never dreamed a company of mine should come to this! It's terrible, it's disgusting, it's so *ugly!*"

For, every morning, on parade, Major Oliver Spoongurgle would inspect his command minutely: not to see whether their weapons were in working order, of course, since that was the last thing he cared about. But to see whether they had washed behind their ears, and trimmed their mustaches, and combed their hair, and put lavender-water on after they had shaved, and all that sort of thing. When he spotted the bitten nails, his face went so purple that, from the distance, it looked as though the fort was being commanded by a giant plum.

What particular horrible punishment he might have inflicted on them for biting their nails, however, no one shall ever know. For just at that moment, the sentry posted on high lookout called: "PARTY APPROACHING, NORTHEAST QUARTER!" The men began to shake where they stood, sure that they were about to be fallen on by the full force of Chief Sitting Bull, and knowing that Major Oliver Spoongurgle did not have the faintest idea of how to defend them. Suddenly Captain Sam Sutton sprang up the ladder to the ramparts, field glasses to his eyes.

"What is it, Captain?" cried the major nervously.

Slowly, the captain lowered his field glasses.

"Open wagon approaching, sir," he replied. He cleared his throat. "It appears to have a goat in it."

The soldiers gasped with relief.

Major Oliver Spoongurgle jumped in the air and clapped his neat white-gloved hands together.

"My goat!" he cried. "My goat's arrived. Bugler, sound *Open Gates!*"

At which command the company bugler, delighted that he wasn't having to sound *Charge!* or *Man the Ramparts!* or *Watch Out for Indians!* or *Help!,* blew a few high, sweet, brassy notes, and the man on the gate lifted the heavy wooden bar and swung open the two huge doors.

Through the doorway, a minute or so later, as the company presented arms and Major Oliver Spoongurgle raised his beautifully polished sword in salute, trundled a plain wooden wagon pulled by a rather scruffy brown mule.

In the back of this cart stood a mangy gray goat. It chewed with a slow, reflective action that made its straggly little beard waggle from side to side, and idly flicked its scruffy hindquarters with what looked like a piece of old gray string, but was in fact the best it could do in the way of a tail.

And on the seat in front of it, holding the reins of the elderly mule, was a small boy of about ten.

Very, very slowly, Major Oliver Spoongurgle lowered his sword until its point touched the

ground. His face, so recently plum-colored, now faded to the color of cream cheese. His mouth, beneath the immaculate black mustache points, fell open. At last, and not without great difficulty, he managed to force some words between his stricken lips.

"What," he croaked, "is *that?*"

The small boy jumped down from the seat.

"Good morning, Major," he said. "My name is Arthur William Foskett. May I introduce Webster?"

"Webster?" echoed the major faintly.

"The goat," explained Arthur.

Major Oliver Spoongurgle swayed, as if about to faint, and put out a hand toward Captain Sam Sutton for support.

"Goat?" he murmured. "You call that thing, that moldy fleabag, that heap of smelly knitting — you call *that* a goat?"

Arthur looked up at the major, slowly. When he spoke, he spoke very carefully and very politely, but very firmly.

"Webster," he said, "is not only a goat, he is probably the most intelligent goat in the world. He is also an extremely nice goat. He is not a thing, he is not moldy, and he does not have fleas. He may smell a bit different from people" — and here Arthur paused, and sniffed deeply — "because goats do not, as far as I

23

know, use lavender-water, but it is a perfectly proper smell for a goat."

Major Oliver Spoongurgle's face clenched like a fist.

"When I asked for a goat," he said, "I expected something white and beautiful, something smart and dignified, something behind which this elegant company would be proud to march. I also expected it to arrive properly accompanied by a troop of horses and an officer

bearing its pedigree, so that we would know that it was a goat from a good family. Who are you, and where did you get that pile of horribleness?"

Now, Arthur had been brought up to treat everyone he met with respect and politeness. He also recognized that the major *was* a major, even though, on first appearances, he didn't seem to be much of one. So he swallowed any sharp reply he might have made to this further insult concerning Webster, and said, quietly: "As you know, sir, there is a war on at the moment. When your request came for a regimental goat, everyone at regimental headquarters in Fort Peck was a bit busy organizing troop movements and moving cannon and working out battle tactics and all the rest of it. I'm afraid no one had time to sort out a particular goat. In fact, you probably wouldn't have got a goat at all, except that I happened to hear about it, and I thought I ought to do my bit to help out. And as I've known Webster for a long time and know him to be a remarkably nice and intelligent goat, I decided to bring him to you."

It was Captain Sam Sutton's turn to gasp!

"Just a minute, young Arthur!" he exclaimed. "Do you mean to say you've come a hundred miles from Fort Peck *all by yourself?*"

"That's right, sir," replied Arthur.

"Through Indian country?"

"Yes," said Arthur. "It took me five days, or rather nights. That is rather a long time, I know, but I thought it best to travel by dark. The Sioux don't attack at night, you know."

"Yes, I did know," said Captain Sam Sutton, looking at Arthur with considerable respect. "You're a very brave young man. Thank you very much for Webster. Our company will be proud to have him."

"Rubbish!" snapped Major Oliver Spoongurgle. "Nothing of the kind! I'd rather march behind a regimental rat than that thing!"

"But Major," protested the captain, "after Arthur has brought him all this —"

"NOT ANOTHER WORD!" shouted the major.

"And if you wouldn't mind dismissing the men, Sergeant, I really must go and have a bit of a rest. This has all been a great shock to me, you know."

Whereupon Major Oliver Spoongurgle turned on his elegant heel and marched delicately away toward his quarters, dabbing his hankie to his forehead as he went.

The men were dismissed, and went back miserably to their polishing. Captain Sam Sutton put a friendly hand on Arthur's shoulder.

"Sorry about that, Arthur," he said. "I'm afraid the major has rather a lot on his mind at present. You'd better go round to the cookhouse and get some breakfast while we work out what's best for you to do. You'll have to stay, of course. We can't possibly let you go back to Fort Peck, with Sitting Bull liable to swoop down any second."

"I'll take Webster with me if I may, sir," said Arthur, dropping the buck board of the cart and leading the goat onto the parade ground. "He gets pretty hungry, too."

27

"Of course," replied the captain, "and I'll see to it your mule gets fed and quartered with the horses. You'll find the cookhouse around the . . ."

But Webster, who had been sniffing the air very carefully, was already tugging on his lead and scratching at the gravel with his front hoof.

"It's all right, sir," said Arthur. "Webster will find it. He's got a very good nose for things like breakfast."

And, with Arthur nearly tipping over because of Webster's eager tug, the small boy and the goat set off at a trot toward the delicious smell of frying that was issuing in wispy puffs from the tin smokestack of the kitchen.

It says much for tiny Private Bingle's presence of mind that he did not faint when Webster's nose suddenly appeared in his lap. He was sitting on the cookhouse step, staring at the two-hundredth potato he had peeled that morning, when the goat's scruffy muzzle shoved itself onto his knee.

"My goodness!" cried Private Bingle, dropping his peeler. "What's this, then?"

"It's Webster," said Arthur. "Potato peelings are just about his favorite food."

"What a stroke of luck!" exclaimed Private Bingle. "I was just this moment thinking I ought to gather them all up and take them out to the garbage can. Not the nicest job, I don't mind saying."

"Oh, Webster will get rid of them for you," said Arthur, "won't you, Webster?"

At which Webster, who had extraordinarily good manners and had been waiting patiently for a proper invitation, plunged his face into the enormous pile of peelings, and began to chomp.

Arthur and Private Bingle introduced themselves. Arthur explained about the arrival of Webster, and Major Oliver Spoongurgle's reaction. Private Bingle nodded gloomily and explained, in his turn, about Major Oliver Spoongurgle.

"It doesn't surprise me," said Arthur, when he'd finished. "I should imagine *we'll* be confined to the cookhouse, too."

"No doubt about it, I'm afraid," replied Private Bingle. "You're even shorter than I am, so he'll never let *you* near the parade ground, and you know what he thinks about Webster. Still," he went on, brightening, "it's nice and peaceful around here, the food's all right, and nobody bothers us. Come and meet the others."

So, leaving Webster with the pile of peelings, which was going down with amazing speed, Arthur followed Private Bingle into the cookhouse and shook hands with Private Conk and Private Wibbley. He sat down to a huge, steaming plate of fried eggs and hash brown potatoes and fresh sweet corn, and soon forgot his disappointment that Webster's career as a cavalry goat seemed to have ended before it had begun.

"I suppose," said Private Conk, as Arthur pushed back his empty plate, "we could always *paint* Webster white, and make a false tail out of a nice piece of rope, and cut his beard off."

"Yes, and while we're at it," snapped Private Wibbley, glaring up at him, "we could chop your legs off at the knee and glue them onto Bingle's feet, so that you'd both be the same

31

height as everybody else! Just suit old Spoon-gurgle, that would."

"He's right," said Bingle. "Webster's perfectly okay as he is, he'd make an extremely good regimental mascot; it's rotten old Spoon-gurgle who's wrong."

"He can walk on his hind legs," said Arthur.

"Spoongurgle?" inquired Conk, puzzled.

They all stared at him.

"You'll have to forgive Conk," said Private Bingle to Arthur. "It's all on account of his being so tall. It takes ideas twice as long to get up to his brain. It's *Webster* who can walk on his hind legs," he shouted up at Conk, "you big gumboil!"

"Oh," murmured Conk.

"Yes," said Arthur. "I've trained him. It's a hobby of mine. I used to do shows with him at Fort Peck. I used to do card tricks and juggling, and Webster used to walk around on his hind legs."

"Card tricks?" cried Wibbley, clapping his pudgy hands. "Juggling?"

32

In answer, Arthur took four soup dishes from the drainer and, as Private Conk trembled (having a fair idea of what Major Oliver Spoongurgle would do if he heard that one of his precious bone china plates had broken), tossed them in the air so fast that they seemed to turn before the private's amazed eyes into a shimmering white cartwheel!

"I can see you're going to brighten the place up no end," said Private Bingle, as Arthur replaced the plates in their rack, to the enormous relief of Private Conk. "What else can you do, Arthur?"

"Oh, nothing much," replied Arthur, who hated the idea that he might sound boastful, while at the same time wanting to tell the truth. "I can walk on my hands a bit, and do a little ventriloquism, but that's about all."

"What on earth," asked Private Conk, "is ventle, ventro, er . . ."

"Ventriloquism," explained Arthur, "is the method of throwing your voice while at the same time not moving your lips —"

"— so that it looks as if the stove is speaking," said the stove.

The privates gasped!

The privates reeled!

"The stove," shrieked Private Conk. "It spoke!"

"Oh, shut up, Conk!" snapped Bingle.

"Shut up, Conk!" snapped the stove.

"That," cried Private Wibbley, "is the most astounding thing I ever heard, Arthur."

"Oh," murmured Arthur, "it's only a trick. It's easy when you know how. It's not nearly as difficult as . . ."

But what ventriloquism was not as difficult as had to remain a mystery; for at that moment, the bugler blared *Open Gates!* again, and a split second later the four friends heard the clatter of frantic hooves echo around the parade ground.

They sprang through the cookhouse door, past Webster the goat (who was lying in the sun, full of food, blinking happily, and certainly in no mood to go charging around like a mad human), and up to the wooden rails that separated the cookhouse block from the square.

The soldier who leapt from the sweat-glistening horse hurled himself toward Captain Sam Sutton, who had simultaneously run to meet him. He thrust a dispatch case into the officer's hand, and began gesturing excitedly in the direction from which he had come.

The captain tore open the dispatch case, glanced at the papers inside, turned, sprinted up the steps toward Major Oliver Spoongurgle's quarters, and disappeared inside.

"I wonder," said Arthur, "what all that was about."

What it was about, Captain Sam Sutton was at that moment making very plain to Major Oliver Spoongurgle.

"The general's orders are very clear, sir," he said. "The settlement at Beaver Creek has been overrun, and our company is to proceed there immediately and attempt to engage the enemy. May I sound the general alert?"

"Fighting!" muttered the major, who had turned very white. "Fighting, that's all this army ever thinks about! We'll get *filthy!*"

"What?" gasped Captain Sam Sutton.

"Our uniforms, you idiot!" cried the major. "They could get ruined! We shall probably have to fire some of our beautiful cannonballs, we may even, heaven help us" — and here he shuddered — "get blood on our swords, if we're not very careful. And may I remind you, Captain, that we do not even have a proper goat? If you think I'm taking that revolting Webster thing with us, you've got another think coming! I shan't go!"

The captain stared at his commanding officer, and licked dry lips.

"Major, I don't think you understand. These are *orders!* You have no alternative."

Gloomily, Major Oliver Spoongurgle stared at the dispatches. All that polishing going to waste! No goat! And, far worse, there was a good chance they'd run into the enemy, unless he could find a way of avoiding it. *This*, thought the major miserably, was definitely not why he had joined the army. This had nothing to do with strutting about in lovely shiny boots and riding through a town on a big, white horse while people took their hats off and cheered.

But there was nothing he could do about it. Orders were orders.

Major Oliver Spoongurgle sighed heavily.

"Oh, very well," he muttered.

So Captain Sam Sutton saluted hurriedly and left, and gave his orders to the junior officers. Within a very few minutes the bugler had sounded *Muster!* and the entire company assembled on the parade ground in battle order, the guns now hitched to horses, the cannonballs and powder loaded on wagons, the soldiers mounted and ready to ride out.

All except, of course, for the small detail of a dozen men and a corporal left behind to defend the fort. As Major Oliver Spoongurgle came slowly and reluctantly down the steps, his eye fell on them.

"Who are they?" he barked. "Why are they not mounted?"

"Defense detail, sir," replied Captain Sam Sutton.

"Rubbish!" cried the major. "We need every

man we can take. There might be more than one Indian. I'm not going into battle against odds like that, Captain!"

"Very well, then," said the captain, for time was pressing and while they were standing arguing, Sitting Bull was on the move. "We'll have to take the cookhouse detail and the boy with the goat. We can't possibly leave them to —"

"Are you out of your mind?" yelled the major. "Mess up the whole look of the thing with those three misshapen louts and that midget and his walking doormat? Bugler, sound the advance!"

There was nothing further that the captain could say. The major was, after all, his superior officer. So, as the bugler blew, the long, blue column began to wind through the gates at a bridle-jingling trot, with the sun glinting off every piece of perfectly polished equipment, and with the great cannon trundling along at the rear. Five pairs of eyes were left behind to watch them go. Even Webster the goat seemed to sense that all was not as it should be, as the troops and horses and guns dwindled in the picture frame of the gateway, leaving only their dust rising slowly on the morning air.

But if Private Conk and Private Bingle and Private Wibbley were trembling beneath their aprons at the dreadful thought of what might happen if the Indians realized that Fort Moccasin was utterly undefended, Arthur had no intention of letting such worries get the better of him.

"Right," he said, putting his hands on his hips and looking around him at the others, "the first thing we'd better do is shut the gate!"

"Very smart!" exclaimed Private Wibbley. "Very smart indeed!"

The other two privates agreed, nodding vigorously. Arthur walked across to the long mirror, looked, and was forced to admit to himself that he did look pretty good in uniform, even if it was only Private Bingle's second-best uniform, cut down to Arthur's size, and Private

Conk's second-best cap, with a pleat taken in at the back so that it sat very snugly on Arthur's head.

"Of course," said Arthur, "it'll only fool the enemy from a considerable distance. I'm a bit short for a U.S. cavalryman."

"Oh, I wouldn't say that," said Private Bingle, who was secretly so delighted to be standing next to a soldier shorter than he was that he almost forgot the terrifying circumstances that had brought it about.

"Not that it matters much, anyhow," said

41

Private Conk, somewhat gloomily, from his great height above them. "Even if we were all twice as big as I am, that still wouldn't scare the enemy off. The Sioux aren't going to turn and run when they see just four soldiers."

"Nonsense!" cried Arthur, realizing that this was no time to be *too* polite. "Don't be a defeatist, Private Conk! It isn't how many we are that counts, it's what we can manage to do. Let's go outside and work out a Plan!"

They marched out into the morning sunshine and into the center of the immaculate parade ground. There can be little doubt that if Major Oliver Spoongurgle had seen these four unmatching uniformed shapes scrunching across his precious gravel, he would have fallen down in a dead faint. But, for Conk and Wibbley and Bingle, it was wonderful to be in cavalry blue again, and out of their aprons. Except, of course, for the one thing that was missing.

"If only," muttered Private Bingle, "we had rifles!"

"Or revolvers!" cried Conk.

42

"Or swords, even!" said Wibbley, slashing at the air with the soup ladle he had brought along, just for something to carry as a weapon.

"Well," said Arthur, "the fact of the matter is that we must make the Indians, if they do attack, *think* we have guns. There wouldn't be any point in throwing potatoes at them or charging them with your broomstick spears. That would be very brave, but it would get us nowhere at all, except dead. It would be worse than useless, in fact, because they'd realize immediately that they were the best weapons we had. No, the most important thing is to make the fort look full of soldiers: we'll have to light

43

fires in all the fireplaces, so that all the chimneys smoke, and we'll have to make as much noise as we can blowing bugles and banging pots and pans together. We'll all have to run along the firing platforms, sticking our heads out at different places, so that it seems as though there are lots of soldiers, and we'll have to keep on shouting at one another, all that sort of thing."

"Stick our heads out?" inquired Private Conk nervously, thinking of the stories he had heard about Sioux marksmen who could shoot a pea off a post from half a mile away.

"Yes," replied Arthur firmly.

"It won't be any use," said Private Bingle. "As soon as they ride toward the fort, they'll realize that nobody is shooting at them, and that will be that."

"Ah," said Arthur, "I've thought about that. We may not have any guns, but we *do* have gunpowder. What we'll do is put little piles of it all along the firing platform, and if the enemy does attack, we'll run along with a burning torch and set them off. The bangs might discourage them."

Private Conk looked down at him.

"It's a good thing you said *might*," he muttered. "I was beginning to think you were crazy."

"The trouble with you, Private Conk," said Arthur sternly, "is you give up too easily."

Private Conk sighed.

"The trouble with *me*," he replied, "is that I'm twice as big a target as anybody else. If you were me, Arthur, you'd worry, too."

The two other privates became very pale at this, and even Webster the goat seemed to sense that the conversation had taken an unsettling turn, and stopped chewing. Arthur, however, merely set his jaw more firmly.

"I don't think we ought to talk about targets," he said briskly. "There's work to be done."

And they began to do it.

The day went rather well, all things considered, and one of the best things about being busy was that the four friends had no time to stop and think about bullets, arrows, tomahawks, and all the rest of it.

They set the little piles of gunpowder according to Arthur's instructions. They kept the fires stoked. They set up a clothesline on the roof of the cookhouse, where it could be seen from outside the fort, to give the impression, from the dozens of pairs of pants they hung on it, that the place was filled to overflowing with soldiers waiting for clean underwear. They also managed to find a number of spare uniforms, which they buttoned up and stuffed with straw. On the collars of these they placed turnips, each turnip painted to look — from a distance — like a face, and they put caps on the turnips. And when this was done they propped the dummies in the firing gaps around the walls of the fort, so that the enemy would think the dummies were real, live soldiers.

When all the work was finished, and evening

46

began to fall, they realized they had managed
to get through at least one day without an In-

dian attack. So they built a big fire in the middle of Major Oliver Spoongurgle's precious parade ground, and they cooked their evening meal on it, because, as Arthur pointed out, if there *were* any Indian scouting parties around, it wouldn't hurt at all to let them see the smoke and flames of a large fire, and even smell the delicious smell of sizzling steaks and hear the crackle of baked potatoes as they jumped and popped in the bright yellow heart of the bonfire.

There would be no way for those Indians to tell that sitting around those roaring flames were just three kitchen-cleaners and a small boy of about ten. Not forgetting, of course, Webster the goat.

And when the meal was finished, they rolled themselves in their thick, blue cavalry blankets

beside the glowing fire, and, knowing that the Sioux would not attack at night, they slept.

They woke as dawn rolled back the darkness.

But it wasn't the silver light in the sky that woke them.

And it wasn't the sudden, sharp bite of the early cold.

And it wasn't the piercing cries of birds rising in the lightening sky.

It was something else.

Arthur, who was a very light sleeper, was the first to hear it. He rolled over, waking Webster the goat, who had been sleeping on his feet and dreaming of potato peel.

He stood up, his hand over Webster's muzzle to keep him quiet, and he listened hard.

There it was again!

A high, looping cry, not quite a coyote's cry, not quite a timber wolf's howl, yet very like them.

He nudged Private Bingle, and when Bingle's eyes snapped open, Arthur put a finger to his friend's lips. Then he moved quickly across and woke the other two.

All four listened.

The strange whoop came again!

"What is it?" whispered Private Bingle.

"I can't be absolutely sure," replied Arthur, quietly and calmly, "but it could very well be Sioux scouts signaling to one another!"

"Oh, heavens!" muttered Private Wibbley.

"B-b-b-b-b-!" stammered Private Conk. "G-g-g-g-g-!"

But whatever it was he wanted to say, his chattering teeth would not allow anything else to get past them.

"You wait here," said Arthur, "and get ready for possible action. You all know what you have to do. I'm going up the ladder to the observation platform."

Whereupon he crossed the parade ground at a silent, tiptoeing run, swung himself up onto the ladder, and began, very swiftly, to climb to the top.

When Arthur reached the observation platform, the landscape that spread out beneath him was so startlingly beautiful that he almost forgot his reason for being there. As the sun broke, golden, over the rim of mountains to the east, the light flowed across the broad sweep of valley, turning the Milk River to a ribbon of pale honey. Arthur thought he had never seen anything quite so peaceful in his entire life. It seemed quite unbelievable that down there, in the soft morning stillness and the gently rising mists, there was a dangerous enemy, waiting its moment to pounce, shrieking and firing, upon Fort Moccasin.

He stared into this unmoving picture, peering through slitted eyes for some tiny sign which would give away the enemy's presence. Nothing stirred, except the odd tawny jackrabbit bouncing across his green field like a furry ball.

Perhaps they weren't there at all? Perhaps the whoop *had* been some mountain animal after all? Perhaps his imagination had . . .

And then he saw them.

A bush moved, a few hundred yards to the left of the fort, and two dark shapes stood there for a second before the bush folded them in again. And, to the right this time, he spotted three more. Sioux scouts, spying out the lie of the fort. And, as the light grew stronger, there,

on the banks of the Milk River a couple of miles to the north, he could just distinguish a darkish mass that wasn't trees or bushes or anything else but a large force of men and horses.

Quickly, Arthur swung himself back onto the ladder and slid to the ground again. The other three looked at him, not daring to ask.

Arthur just nodded.

"I should think they're only waiting for the light to get full," he said quietly.

But for once Arthur was wrong.

Because, even as he said it, a far, faint rumble caught their ears; and this time those ears were in no doubt whatever.

"They're c-c-c-c-c-!" cried Private Conk, grabbing Private Bingle.

"Yes," muttered Private Wibbley, "they're coming, all right!"

"Right!" shouted Arthur, who had no intention of standing there trembling and stuttering. "Get to the firing platforms! Sound the bugles! Shout as loudly as you can!"

Not, Arthur thought, even as he ran himself,

that shouting and bugling was going to do any good now. The Indians had scouted the fort. They had not been put off by the signs of life or the dummies propped against the embrasures, and would probably have attacked even if the cavalry had still been there in full strength. Still, Arthur said to himself as he reached his position on the firing platform and lit his torch, you have to do what you can . . .

He glanced over the top of the wall, and gasped! That same view, so peaceful five minutes earlier, was now alive with charging, whooping men, bearing down in a great, billowing line of horses that seemed to fill the landscape from end to end. The noise of the privates' bugles was utterly washed away by the thunder and the shrieking of the Indian attack. And now, here and there along the line, Arthur noticed, with a cold clenching of his stomach, the puffs of smoke and stabs of flame that spat from the guns the Sioux were firing as they rode!

Beside him, a dummy flew backwards, the air filled with whirling straw from the terrible

54

bullet, and slowly tumbled, broken, to the ground below.

"NOW!" yelled Arthur, though the others

probably couldn't hear, and touched his torch to the little piles of gunpowder.

They did not really bang, for powder has to be compressed into a gunbarrel before it will explode properly, but they went up in great WHOOSHES, and smoke and flame burst from twenty places along the wall; the effect was really not too different from that of a line of cannon firing.

As luck would have it, the general noise and excitement of the charge was such that the Indians did not immediately notice that the thunder of guns was missing. They had, after all, been prepared for firing from the walls, and when they saw the smoke and flames leap up from the whole length of Fort Moccasin, they naturally reeled and reined and swerved, and the horses, startled by all this, lurched into one another, so that several riders were hurled to the ground. Other warriors, seeing this happen, automatically assumed that their companions had been struck by cannonballs or bullets, and they, too, were thrown into confusion and broke stride, some pulling up, some bearing away to left and right, until at last the line was not a line at all, but rather a ragged mess of men and horses in disconnected groups that had suddenly stopped going forward.

Whereupon three or four of the Sioux leaders whooped a special signal that was taken up from group to group, and the whole company of Indians wheeled about and began to gallop furiously back the way they had come.

On the ramparts, Arthur and his three grown-up friends, their faces blackened by powder smoke, watched them go.

"Hurrah!" cried Private Conk, hardly believing his eyes. "We've beaten them off! Three cheers for Arthur!"

But Arthur shook his head.

"I'm afraid not," he said. "If there had only

been a few of them, it might have worked. They might have calculated what they thought were the odds, and decided not to take the risk. But the Sioux are very brave, and extraordinarily tough. Right now their leaders are probably planning their next charge and reckoning that enough of them will get past our guns this time to smash down the gates, or swarm over the walls, and take the fort." Here Arthur gave a grim little smile. "And we know they'll get past *our* guns without much trouble, don't we?"

The happy relief had drained out of his friends' faces while Arthur was talking. But they were soldiers, still; so Private Wibbley set

his jaw and said: "Right, lads, then it's up and at 'em with potatoes and forks!"

Arthur looked at him, feeling very proud that Private Wibbley was his friend. But what he said was: "It's just possible it may not come to that."

They stared at him.

"I have," said Arthur, "an Emergency Plan. I didn't mention it before, because I didn't want anyone to start worrying that we might *need* an Emergency Plan. But now it looks very much as though we do, and I'm going to try it."

"What is it?" cried Private Conk desperately, thinking that anything was better than facing several hundred Sioux warriors armed only with a potato. "What shall we do?"

"Not you," replied Arthur, glancing quickly through a firing slot to make sure the Sioux hadn't yet turned to begin their second charge. "The Plan is just for me and Webster!"

Hearing his name, Webster, who had been waiting patiently in the parade ground, pricked up his shaggy ears. But they weren't pricked anywhere near as high as Private Bingle's!

"*You and Webster?*" he exclaimed. "What on earth . . . ?"

"We'll need a white flag of truce," said Arthur calmly, "and you three will have to pull the gate open for me."

"You're going," whispered Private Conk hoarsely, "out *there?*"

"I'm going," replied Arthur, "to talk to the Indians!"

One minute later, as the three privates stared in terror from the open gates of Fort Moccasin, Arthur William Foskett and Webster the goat walked slowly into the sun toward the point where the Sioux were preparing to restart their attack.

Arthur was carrying a white pillowcase tied to a broomstick, and his heart, for all his amazing bravery, was beating in his ears with the clatter of a tin drum.

As Arthur approached, a brave clutched the arm of the Sioux chief beside him, and pointed.

The chief stared!

It was a tiny cavalryman and a goat. What did it mean? Why was this peculiar couple coming toward him under a white flag of truce?

But he was an experienced warrior who ignored nothing just because it seemed extraordinary, and he always respected a flag of truce. He nudged his white pony with his knees, and slowly went forward, with three or four of his braves, to meet Arthur and Webster.

Now, Arthur, for all his many talents and skills, did not speak the Sioux language; but he reckoned that a great Sioux chief with hundreds of warriors under his command who had been fighting the army for many years would probably speak a little English.

So it proved.

The small group of warriors stopped. Arthur and Webster stopped. They faced one another for a few moments, silently. Then Arthur put up his right hand, this being the sign the Indians used to show they did not carry a weapon and came only to talk, and said: "Good morning."

The chief put up his hand, and said: "Good morning, mister."

And then Webster the goat got up on his two hind legs, and said: "Good morning, O great and mighty chief of the Sioux!"

Well, you can just imagine what effect *that* had on the Indians! Their horses reared up in astonishment, of course, but they weren't half as astonished as their riders, I can tell you! In

fact, the braves who accompanied the chief cried out, leapt from their horses, and fell to their knees on the ground in front of Webster.

For the Sioux were a people of many deep and, to us, strange beliefs, and many peculiar superstitions. Perhaps the most important among these was that their gods inhabited strange forms, and could speak to them in the wind and in the water and in the thunder. And what was more natural than to believe, when you heard a goat on its hind legs speak,

that a god had chosen this form to address you?

The chief did not dismount, because he *was* a chief, and for his people's sake was cautious in what he said and did. Although, of course, he was deeply shaken by Webster; he stared at him, and when he spoke, his voice was low and shaky.

"Do you speak to me, Chief Cloud-That-Dances of the mighty Sioux people? Or is it the wind that plays tricks in my ears?"

Webster did a little circular walk before replying.

"O bravest of the brave, Chief Cloud-That-Dances," said Webster, in a deep and thrilling voice, "to whom should I speak, I who am Walking Goat, messenger of the gods, if not to you, the great leader of his people?"

Chief Cloud-That-Dances slowly dismounted at this. He raised his great head to the sky and shook his rifle high above it, and called out, in his own language: "IT IS TRUE! THE GOD-GOAT TALKS!"

The warriors behind him, hearing his shout, set up the same great echoing cry: "THE GOD-GOAT TALKS! THE GOD-GOAT TALKS TO CLOUD-THAT-DANCES!"

The chief lowered his rifle, and murmured to Webster: "What message do you bring me, O great Walking Goat?"

"I have lived with the pony-soldiers," replied Webster, "and I know they do not want this war with the Sioux nation. This is also the wish of the gods, who ask Chief Cloud-That-Dances to return in peace to his people and settle his arguments with the white man without the spilling of blood."

Chief Cloud-That-Dances nodded gravely.

"I shall heed the advice of the gods, O great Walking Goat," he said. He beckoned his kneeling braves to rise and remount, and slowly the little group rode back to the waiting Sioux army. That army in its turn slowly wheeled its horses' heads around to face north again, and began to move back across the Milk River.

Arthur and Webster stood alone, watching them go. Finally, they too turned and, with Webster once more on all fours, walked back across the green plain to Fort Moccasin.

When Major Oliver Spoongurgle rode into Fort Moccasin at the head of his company on the following day, he was a very different man from the one who had ridden out two days before.

True, the first order he gave was for everyone to go in *immediately* and have a bath and put on clean uniforms and shave and splash their faces with lavender-water, so he wasn't *that* different. But the main point was that he was smiling, and joking, and slapping people on the back, and when I tell you that three of

those people were Privates Bingle, Wibbley, and Conk, you'll understand how great a change had come over Major Oliver Spoongurgle.

The reason for this was not only that the war was over — something, it must be said, that the major had learned the evening before from a special messenger who had had great difficulty in catching up with the Spoongurgle company, since it had been riding so fast in the *opposite* direction from the enemy — but that it was over because of a peace that Chief Cloud-That-Dances had made with the garrison at Fort Moccasin. When the messenger had told him the news, the major had felt there had been some mistake, since he couldn't for the life of him remember that there *was* a garrison at Fort Moccasin.

But, bit by bit, the story of the small boy who could throw his voice, and the goat who could walk on two legs, and the three cookhouse cleaners who had held off an Indian attack with puffs of smoke pieced itself together until Major Oliver Spoongurgle was beside himself with delight. Congratulations were pouring in from other companies and other forts, telling him what a splendid leader he must be to have such brilliant and daring men and goats under his command.

And when word leaked out to him, as he was riding back to the fort in the morning, that there was A Very Strong Possibility that he would be made a colonel for this, Major Oliver Spoongurgle nearly fell off his horse for joy. He already saw himself in his gorgeous colonel's uniform at the head of an entire regiment of impeccably marching men.

Which was why, as soon as he had shaved and dressed, he summoned the five heroes, including Webster the goat, to his quarters.

"Wonderful!" shouted the major, beaming at them. "Splendid! What a fine body of men!"

They didn't know quite what to say to this, since they were all, as you know, modest fellows, and certainly not at all used to Spoongurgle compliments.

So none of them said anything, except poor Private Conk, who was so embarrassed he could only mumble: "I'm sorry I'm so tall, sir."

To which Major Oliver Spoongurgle immediately replied: "Nonsense, Conk! You're the

71

perfect height for your size! I've always said so, haven't I, Captain?"

Captain Sam Sutton cleared his throat and looked at the ceiling.

"And as for that goat," continued the major cheerily, "as soon as I set eyes on him, I knew he was just the goat for us! What bearing! What style!"

"Thank you," said Webster.

The major threw back his head and roared with laughter.

"Arthur, my boy, you must be the best ventriloquist in all the world!" he shouted.

"Oh, it's very easy, really," said Arthur.

"Rubbish!" retorted the major. His face grew thoughtful. "Of course, we'll have to get you your own uniform. Can't have you leading Webster around in Bingle's old jacket, can we?"

"Leading Webster?" said Arthur. "Oh, I'm afraid I won't be able to stay. I have to go home this afternoon. They're expecting me."

They all looked at him, suddenly silent and suddenly sad.

"I was forgetting," murmured Major Oliver Spoongurgle. "You turned out to be such a splendid soldier, I'd quite forgotten you weren't really in the cavalry at all."

"He *was*, though," said Captain Sam Sutton, quietly. "If only for a couple of days. And the cavalry was very lucky to have him, too!"

"Hear, hear!" cried the major. "It just goes to show that appearances aren't everything, I suppose."

The others gazed at him in amazement. Major Oliver Spoongurgle was a changed man all right, of that there was no doubt at all! As for the major himself, he stood up, saluted Arthur smartly, and shook his hand.

"You'll come back and see us, though," he said, "won't you?"

"Oh, yes," said Webster the goat, "he'll certainly do that!"